JUDY MOODY AND FRIENDS

Judy Moody and the Missing Mood Ring

Megan McDonald

illustrated by Erwin Madrid

based on the characters
created by Peter H. Reynolds

CANDLEWICK PRESS

For Jahkai and Najilah

MM

To my daughter, Lena

EM

Text copyright © 2022 by Megan McDonald
Illustrations copyright © 2022 by Peter H. Reynolds
Judy Moody font copyright © 2003 by Peter H. Reynolds

Judy Moody®. Judy Moody is a registered trademark of Candlewick Press, Inc.
Stink®. Stink is a registered trademark of Candlewick Press, Inc.
Portions of this text were previously published in *Judy Moody, Girl Detective*,
copyright © 2010 by Megan McDonald.

First edition 2022

Library of Congress Catalog Card Number pending
ISBN 978-1-5362-0975-4 (hardcover)
ISBN 978-1-5362-1014-9 (paperback)

22 23 24 25 26 27 CCP 10 9 8 7 6 5 4 3 2 1

Printed in Shenzhen, Guangdong, China

This book was typeset in ITC Stone Informal.
The illustrations were created digitally.

Candlewick Press
99 Dover Street
Somerville, Massachusetts 02144

www.candlewick.com

CONTENTS

CHAPTER 1
The Secret in the Old Attic

Judy Moody loved to read. She loved
to read mysteries. And who was
the best solver of mysteries in the
whole wide world? Nancy Drew, Girl
Detective, of course.

Judy's top three favorite things
about Nancy Drew were:

1) She was a teenager.

2) She was a Girl Detective.

3) She always carried a handy-dandy bobby pin, just in case she had to open a locked door or something.

Judy Moody was walking home from the library with her nose in a Nancy Drew book, *The Scarlet Slipper Mystery*, when—*BAM!*—she ran smack-dab into a girl. A girl carrying a giant stack of library books. The books went flying. *OOPS!*

"Sorry!" Judy and the girl said at the exact same time. Judy helped pick up the books. She picked up *The Secret in the Old Attic, The Hidden Staircase* . . . "Nancy Drew!" she said.

"Yes, I'm freaky for Nancy Drew," said the girl. "Can you tell?"

"I'm freaky for Nancy Drew, too!" said Judy. "I'm reading all fifty-six classic Nancy Drew books."

"Hey, I think I know you," said
the girl. "We were in that big Book
Quiz Blowout together. Aren't you
Judy Moody, Book Quiz Whiz, from
Virginia Dare Elementary?"

Judy nodded. "That's right. I
remember you now! You're the fourth-
grader from Braintree Academy who
reads Harry Potter. You're Mighty
Fantaskey!"

"That's me," said Mighty. "Right now I'm into mysteries."

"I love mysteries!" said Judy Moody. "I wish I could solve a real-life mystery."

"That would be fantastic!" said Mighty. "Like a mystery with a stolen pony. Or a rare Chinese vase."

"Or a glowing green man," said Judy.

"Or a secret code in an old letter," said Mighty.

"I'd solve it just like Nancy Drew, Girl Detective, does," said Judy. She tapped the side of her head. "With brains."

"And bravery," said Mighty.

"And bobby pins!" said Judy. They both cracked up.

Before you could say *"Scarlet Slipper Mystery"* three times fast, Judy Moody and Mighty Fantaskey had planned a playdate at Mighty's house for the very next day.

***

Judy's mom pulled up outside Mighty Fantaskey's. It was a tall house that had purple front steps, a porch covered in vines, and a tower on one side like a castle.

"That looks like a haunted house!" said Stink, leaning over. "No way would I ever go in there."

The house *did* look way old and spooky. Judy Moody rubbed her mood ring. It helped her pluck up her courage. Nancy Drew had tons of

pluck. Nancy Drew had oodles and oodles of courage.

Stink could tell that Judy seemed nervous. "Let me see your ring," he said. "What color is it?"

Judy showed him the ring.

"What does brown stand for? *Scared Out of Your Pants*?"

Judy glanced at her mood ring.
"Not brown, Stink.
Amber." Amber
was for *Nervous*.
Amber was
for *Not So Sure*.
Amber seemed to
whisper, *Never Go Inside Haunted
Houses*.

"For your information, Stink,
amber stands for *Tons of Fun*. RARE!"

"You mean *scare*?" said Stink.

Judy took her time getting out of
the car. She watched Mom and Stink
drive off. She climbed the purple
steps and knocked on the front door.
Mighty opened the door.

Judy stepped inside.

The first thing Judy noticed was a fancy ceiling light in the front hall. It was swinging back and forth.

"Do you see that?" Judy said to Mighty.

"See what?" Mighty asked, looking puzzled.

"Uh, never mind." *Weird.*

"So," asked Mighty, "what do you want to do?"

Just then, from out of nowhere, spooky music drifted into the room. Mighty didn't even seem to hear the music. Judy felt goose bumps up and down her back. *Weird and weirder.*

"How old is this house anyway?" Judy asked.

"Super old," said Mighty. "A

hundred years old, at least."

Old enough to have skeletons in the basement, Judy thought. *Or ghosts in the attic.*

As if Mighty Fantaskey could read Judy's mind, she said, "Hey! I have an idea. Want to explore the attic? It's creepy and spooky, but in a Nancy Drew way."

Judy followed Mighty up the stairs, dragging her feet a bit.

In the second-floor hallway, Mighty yanked a rope hanging from the ceiling. The ceiling opened and down came an unfolding staircase, like a ladder, that led into a dark hole. A blast of cold, stale air came tumbling out.

Judy checked her mood ring. Cloudy gray. Gray was for *Goose Bumps.* Gray was for *Shivers.* Gray was for *I'm a Scaredy-Cat.*

Creak. Croak. Creak. The two girls climbed each creaky step on the creaky ladder to the dark attic.

Mighty pulled a string. A single, dim bulb came on.

Judy knew just how Nancy Drew felt whenever she said, "Jeepers!"

The attic was full of cobwebs. The attic was full of shadows. The attic was full of junk covered in million-year-old dust: chairs, rolls of carpet, old-timey paintings, a cracked mirror.

In front of the cracked mirror stood something big and hairy and scary. *Just an old fur coat*, Judy told herself.

Just then, the furry thing turned and looked straight at Judy!

"*AGHHHH!*" Judy screamed and made a beeline for the exit.

"Judy! Wait! Stop!" Mighty called after her.

But Judy didn't wait. She didn't stop. Judy scrambled down the ladder, ran down the second-floor hall, then flew down the stairs past the spooky music, under the swinging light, out the front door, and all the way home without stopping once.

CHAPTER 2
The Case of the Three Bs

Back at home, Judy pulled Mouse the cat closer. She felt more than a teeny bit bad for running out on Mighty so fast, but she was glad to be safe in her own top bunk.

Judy tried not to think about haunted houses. She tried not to think about swinging lights and spooky music. She tried not to think about furry monsters or hairy creatures.

Hard as she tried, though, she, Judy Moody, was still in a shivery, quivery mood. A tingle-up-your-spine mood. *What color is that on my mood ring?* she wondered. She looked at her hand to check.

Hello! Her mood ring! It wasn't there. It was missing. As in G-O-N-E *gone*!

When had she last seen it? She couldn't remember. At breakfast? Before soccer? At the library? In the car with Stink?

Stink!

Judy Moody, aka Judy Drewdy,
went to find her Number One Suspect.
She found her little brother in the
kitchen, karate-chopping a banana.

Judy turned her flashlight on Stink.
"Where's my mood ring?" she asked.

Startled, Stink held a hand up. "Honest to pizza! I did NOT steal your mood ring!" he said.

Judy Moody, Girl Detective, narrowed her eyes at Stink. "Then why is your other hand behind your back?"

"I didn't want you to tell Mom and Dad that I was playing with my food."

"Show me."

Stink held up his other hand. It was a slimy, banana-y mess. No ring in sight.

Judy then pointed to Stink's pocket. "Why is there a lump in your pocket shaped exactly like a ring?"

"It's my Captain MagNeato Secret Decoder Ring."

"Prove it."

Stink reached into his pocket with his non-banana hand and pulled out his Captain MagNeato Secret Decoder Ring.

"Rats," said Judy.

"You had your mood ring on in the car on the way to that haunted house," said Stink.

"You mean Mighty Fantaskey's house?"

"Yep. We checked it, remember? It was brown for tons of scare. I mean fun."

"*Amber*, Stink. It was amber."

"Whatever. I didn't touch your ring. I only looked at it. Then you looked at it. Maybe you lost it at Mighty's house."

Wait just a Nancy Drew minute!

This was turning out to be exactly like . . . Nancy Drew mystery number two, *The Hidden Staircase*. Nancy goes to a creepy mansion, sees the creepy ceiling light swinging, hears creepy music, finds a creepy hidden staircase, and sees a creepy, hairy gorilla at the window.

Mighty Fantaskey's house was haunted after all!

She, Judy Moody, had to go back there. She had to go back to get her ring. She had to go back to solve the Mystery of the Missing Mood Ring.

But that meant going back to the haunted house.

WWNDD? What Would Nancy Drew Do?

Judy ran to Mom's room and found a bobby pin in her dresser. She tucked the bobby pin into her mess of hair, just in case.

Now she had three important things, just like Nancy Drew.

Brains.

Bravery.

And a bobby pin.

CHAPTER 3
The Clue in the Floorboard

Judy rode her bike to Mighty Fantaskey's house. She climbed the purple steps. She knocked on the door (three times for good luck).

Mighty looked happy to see Judy. "I'm glad you came back," said Mighty. "You still want to be friends, right?"

"Of course!" said Judy. "But I think I lost my mood ring in your house."

"I haven't seen it," said Mighty. "But if you want to come in, we can look for it." Mighty opened the door wide.

Judy wanted to find her mood ring, but her feet wouldn't move just thinking about stepping back into the spooky house.

"Don't you want to come in?" Mighty asked with a gleam in her eye.

Judy leaned in and whispered, "I think your house might be haunted."

Mighty's eyes got very big. Mighty's eyes began to twinkle again. Then she leaned her head back and howled like a hyena. "I got you, Judy Moody! I got you so good!"

"You mean . . . all that spooky stuff was just a big fat fake-out?" Judy asked.

Mighty nodded. "I'm sorry! I didn't mean to scare you for real."

"Wow," Judy breathed. "I thought I was the Princess of Pranks. But you are the Queen!"

"When you wished for a mystery to solve, I got the idea to spook you from reading *The Hidden Staircase.*"

"It *is* just like *The Hidden Staircase*," said Judy.

"I thought you might figure it out right away since you're a Nancy Drew nut like me."

"Now you have to tell me how you did it," said Judy.

"I asked my brother to jump on his bed upstairs to make the ceiling light swing. He also played some creepy music. Then he sneaked up into the attic super-quick, wearing his gorilla costume, just like in the book."

"Rare!" said Judy.

"You cracked the case, Judy Moody," said Mighty. "Mystery solved."

"Not quite," said Judy. "There's still

a *real* mystery to solve." Judy held up her bare, no-mood-ring hand. "The Mystery of the Missing Mood Ring."

"Oh, right. Where should we look first?" asked Mighty.

Judy stepped inside. "We have to think. Rule Number One of solving mysteries is to use our brains."

Mighty thought it over. "When do you last remember seeing it on your hand?"

"I know I checked my ring before I got out of the car." Judy thought some more. "I remember checking it again when we were about to go up the hidden stairs into the attic." That's when her mood ring had turned gray for *Goose Bumps*.

"Maybe it fell off in the attic," said Mighty.

The attic! Even though the attic was gorilla-free now, it was still spooky.

Climbing the stairs, Judy felt her heart going *thump, thump, thump.* But Rule Number Two of solving mysteries was to be brave.

She gulped in a big brave breath.

Judy and Mighty crawled on their
hands and knees across the attic floor.
They searched every nook and crack
and cranny for the missing mood
ring. *Where was it?*

"I guess my mood ring is not *in the
mood* to be found," said Judy.

Just then, she placed her hand on a loose floorboard. The other end popped up. She lifted her hand. The board went down. She pressed. The board went up.

"Hold on," said Judy. Rule Number Three of solving mysteries: try the bobby pin. She plucked the bobby pin from her hair and used it to pry up and remove the loose board all the way.

Under the loose board was . . . a way-cool, for-real, secret compartment!

"Wow! A secret compartment!" said Judy. "Nancy Drew would be proud."

"It's just like in *The Secret in the Old Lace*," said Mighty.

"For real? I haven't read that one."

"They find an old letter written in French under a loose floorboard."

Mighty shined a flashlight into the space under the floorboard. Judy peered in. "My ring!" she shouted, dusting it off and sliding it onto her finger. It turned purple for *Joyful, On Top of the World.*

"You were right. It must have happened yesterday when I saw your brother in that costume and got scared. I guess it flew off and fell through a crack."

Mighty shined her flashlight into the secret compartment again. "Hey, what's this?" She picked something up and blew on it. A cloud of dust cleared. A piece of paper. A note! An old-timey letter!

The letter was in a secret code.

OLLP RM GSV IZUGVIH.

Signed, Nancy Drew's biggest fan,
Alice Sutherland
December 29, 1930

"Alice in Wonderland left us a secret code from 1930?" Judy screeched.

"Not Alice in Wonderland. Alice *Sutherland.* She must have been a real girl who lived in this old house way back then! She read Nancy Drew books, too. How great is that? Just think—she left this note for us to find someday. It's like a ninety-year-old mystery."

"That's older than my grandma Lou!"

Judy stared at the secret code. It was a classic reverse alphabet code. "I get it. The letter *A* stands for the letter *Z*. The whole alphabet is backward." The girls got pencils and together they worked out the code.

LOOK IN THE RAFTERS.
Judy and Mighty searched the
rafters. "I think I see something!" said
Mighty, reaching up.

She pulled down a musty, dusty old book with a dark-blue cover. With Judy looking over her shoulder, Mighty Fantaskey looked at the cover. "I can't believe it!" said Mighty. "Nancy Drew mystery number two. *The Hidden Staircase*! It's like the one I got from the library, only way old."

Holy macaroni! Judy barely dared to breathe.

"I bet this is one of the first Nancy Drew books *ever*." Mighty opened the book. "Look! The girl Alice wrote something in fancy handwriting."

Judy peered over Mighty's shoulder and read the inscription aloud.

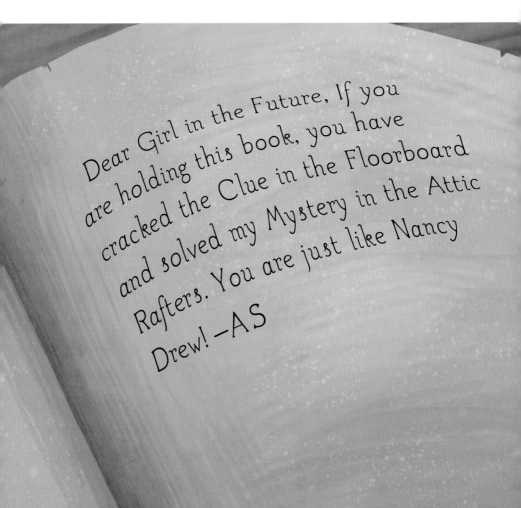

Dear Girl in the Future, If you are holding this book, you have cracked the Clue in the Floorboard and solved my Mystery in the Attic Rafters. You are just like Nancy Drew! —AS

"Same-same!" said Judy, grinning at Mighty.

Together, Girl Detectives Judy Moody and Mighty Fantaskey had solved a ninety-year-old mystery. *The Clue in the Floorboard.* And all it took was the Three Bs: *Brains, Bravery,* and a *Bobby pin*!

And one F. F for *Friends*!

Jeepers!